Special Delivery for Wynnie

There was a knock on the front door. Wynnie pulled herself out of the chair and opened the door. The porch was empty. She stepped out and looked both ways. No one was in sight. Wynnie was about to close the door when she saw it.

A brown box sat on the top step. Wynnie picked it up and carried it inside.

She looked closely at the box, turning it one way and then another. "That's funny," she said. "It didn't come through the mail."

"Well, it didn't just appear on the step," said Mrs. Cadwell.

"Yes," said Wynnie. "It *did.* It just appeared on the step. But it isn't for us. It's for someone named 'Annabelle Dupree.' Hopping toad this really *is* mysterious."

The Birthday Wish Mystery

by Faye Couch Reeves
illustrated by Marilyn Mets

little rainbow®
Troll Associates

To my Mom and Dad with love and thanks.
—*F.C.R.*

Text copyright © 1994 by Faye Couch Reeves.

Illustrations copyright © 1994 by Troll Associates, Inc.

Published by Troll Associates, Inc. Little Rainbow is a trademark of Troll Associates.

Printed in the United States of America.

10   9   8   7   6   5   4   3   2

Library of Congress Cataloging-in-Publication Data

Reeves, Faye Couch.
     The birthday wish mystery / by Faye Couch Reeves; illustrated by Marilyn Mets.
        p.   cm.
ISBN 0-8167-3530-1 (lib. bdg.)   ISBN 0-8167-3531-X (pbk.)
[1. Mystery and detective stories.]   I. Mets, Marilyn, ill.   II. Title.
PZ7.R2559Bi   1994   [FIC]—dc20   94-18348

1

The Birthday Wish

It was a dark and stormy night.

All right, it *wasn't* a dark and stormy night. Wynnie Cadwell just *wished* it were a dark and stormy night, full of thunder and shivers. She wished she could feel goose bumps prickle her arms. She wished her hair would stand on end in fright! She wished it were *anything* but high noon on a Saturday in Linton, Ohio, the most boring little town in the country!

For three long months, Wynnie and her mother had lived in the tiny town of Linton. It wasn't fair. So what if her parents were getting a divorce? She wasn't divorcing her father. And Wynnie loved adventure and mystery. The city where Wynnie used to live was full of adventure and mystery. Linton was not.

Linton was as slow as frozen syrup and as plain as a bread sandwich.

But there was the wish! Almost a year ago Wynnie

1

had leaned over eight birthday candles, closed her eyes and made a wish. "A *real* mystery to solve," she had said to herself. She remembered how the heat from the candles had tickled her chin. "I wish I had a *real* mystery to solve."

Soon it would be her ninth birthday. Wynnie had almost given up waiting for her wish. Then, that very morning, the thought had come to her! Mysteries do not just happen. You have to go out and find them. It was going to take a real detective to find a mystery in boring old Linton. So a real detective was what Wynnie was going to be!

Now, Wynnie stood at the corner of First Street and Maple Avenue. She was looking at Linton through rose-colored sunglasses. Wynnie was as excited as a dog on the scent of a bone. "All I have to do," she said to herself, *"is find that bone."*

Wynnie was wearing a disguise, of course. Her red hair was hidden under a beat-up baseball cap. On her feet she wore blue high-top sneakers for running like a rabbit, stopping on a dime, and walking like a cat. But, best of all, her mother's old raincoat hung all the way to her ankles. Wynnie thought it made the old Wynnie invisible. All Linton could see now was Wynnie Cadwell, mysterious stranger!

"Why, hello, Wynnie," said a voice.

Wynnie looked up, startled, into the face of Mrs. Prescott, mayor of Linton.

"Don't you look sweet today," said Mrs. Prescott, peering at Wynnie through her thick glasses.

"Sweet?" asked Wynnie. "I look *sweet*? Don't I look mysterious, daring . . . different?"

"No," said Mrs. Prescott. "You look just like your dear mother when she was your age."

"Well, hangnails and flat tires!" mumbled Wynnie. Why did Wynnie have to move to the place where her mother had grown up? There were no mysteries, no secrets, no disguises in this town! There wasn't even a pizza parlor in Linton. That's how bad it was.

Being a detective is terrible when there is nothing to detect, thought Wynnie.

"What are you doing, dear?" asked Mrs. Prescott. "Are you waiting for one of your friends?"

"No," said Wynnie, pushing her hands into the pockets of the raincoat. "I'm very careful about the friends I choose," she told Mrs. Prescott seriously. "I want friends who like mystery and adventure. I need a friend I can count on to stick with me during a really tough adventure. If I ever *find* a mystery, that is. So I really don't have any friends, yet."

"That's good," said Mrs. Prescott, adjusting her hearing aid.

4

"That's good," Wynnie muttered disgustedly. "I think I'm getting a wart," she announced loudly.

Mrs. Prescott looked down her nose at Wynnie. "Oh, no," she said, smiling. "I have a wonderful cure for warts, though. An old family secret. It has to do with a full moon and swamp water."

Wynnie blinked at Mrs. Prescott in surprise. "Uh, thanks," said Wynnie. "But, uh, I was just kidding. Ha-ha."

"Now that I really look at you," said Mrs. Prescott, "I can see that *is* an interesting outfit you have on." She looked all the way down to Wynnie's blue high-tops.

"It's a disguise," said Wynnie. "Good detectives, like me, always use disguises. Raincoats and dark glasses and hats."

"Really?" said Mrs. Prescott. "Why is that?"

"We want to keep everyone guessing. A disguise is like . . . a brown paper bag," Wynnie said, warming up. "You can't see what's inside. Have you ever seen a detective walking down the street?"

"No," admitted Mrs. Prescott.

"See? It works," Wynnie told her.

"It's been nice seeing you, dear, but I must run." Mrs. Prescott smiled at Wynnie. "You have a nice day."

Wynnie watched as Mayor Prescott hurried away. "Hog's breath and toads! I don't *want* to have a nice

day! I want to have a *mysterious* day, a *dangerous* day!"
Wynnie sighed. "I might as well go home."

She shuffled along, her eyes on the sidewalk in front of her. Nothing was working. The disguise was a disaster. The mystery was, well, a mystery. If her dad were here, he'd know what to do.

She could still talk to her father on the phone, but it wasn't the same. Just last night he'd been talking about her birthday. Her birthday! Just thinking about it made Wynnie see red—and it had nothing to do with the rose-colored sunglasses she wore.

Wynnie still couldn't believe he wouldn't be there. It was going to be her ninth birthday. A ninth birthday only happens once in a person's life. Wynnie's father would not be there for hers.

No dad. And no birthday wish. She was running out of time. If last year's wish didn't come true before this year's birthday . . . Wynnie hated to think what it might mean. Maybe she'd never get another wish again. Wynnie stuffed her hands deeper into the pockets of the raincoat.

Wynnie had broken the golden rule about birthday wishes. She had told her father about the mystery wish. He'd grinned and said, "That's my girl! A chip off the old block!"

"I never should have told anyone my wish," sighed

Wynnie. She scuffed at a rock with her foot. It bounced into the grass and clover between the sidewalk and the street. Wynnie stopped. Clover! She dropped to her knees to take a closer look. Suddenly Wynnie had a wonderful idea. A four-leaf clover could be right there in front of her nose!

If she found one, that would mean good luck. Good luck might mean her birthday wish would come true after all.

Wynnie pulled out clover after clover. "Three," she muttered, "Three, three, *two*!" Wynnie threw that one to the side in disgust. "Just one more," she said to herself. "Then I'm giving up!" She closed her eyes and pulled. She opened her eyes . . . and found herself staring at a four-leaf clover.

"Wow," she said. "This is a sign. Good luck! A mystery," she whispered. "Maybe we'll move back to the city! Maybe my dad will move to Linton!" Anything, everything seemed possible!

Wynnie was still sitting on the sidewalk, celebrating, when a pair of pink tennis shoes appeared on the sidewalk in front of her. Wynnie looked up at none other than Boomer Balinski.

Boomer Balinski sat across the aisle from Wynnie in Mrs. Paine's fourth-grade class. Today, as always, Boomer was dressed in pink from head to toe. Over one shoulder hung a prissy, pink purse. It even had a pink ruffle.

Wynnie shuddered. Not Boomer Balinski, she thought. Not again! She followed Wynnie everywhere, lately, like a little, pink fly.

Wynnie looked down at her four-leaf clover. "You're not working," she muttered.

Wynnie stood up and faced Boomer with a heavy heart. It wasn't that Wynnie didn't want friends. She did. But Boomer Balinski would never be the mysterious, adventurous, or even just interesting friend Wynnie was looking for.

Wynnie had tried to be nice. She didn't want to hurt Boomer's feelings, but Boomer was still following her around! Wynnie tucked the four-leaf clover safely in her pocket and pushed up her sleeves. No more Miss Nice, she thought.

Boomer smiled. "Hi, Wynnie," she said, in her whispery voice.

Wynnie looked at her wrist. "Oh, wow," she said. "Look at the time! I have to go!"

Boomer sighed. "You're *always* in a hurry. Anyway, how do you know what time it is? You're not wearing a watch!"

"It's a freckle past a hair and I'm a very busy person," said Wynnie, pushing past Boomer.

"Wynnie," called Boomer. "I have to talk to you!"

"Bye!" Wynnie shouted back over her shoulder.

When she reached 324 First Street, Wynnie stopped and looked at her new home. It was tiny. Tall trees on each side made the house seem even smaller.

Wynnie opened the mailbox and searched through the mail inside. "Bill, bill, ad, bill!" sighed Wynnie. Nothing from her dad. That was the only thing Wynnie looked for in the mailbox. "Oh well," said Wynnie. "The good luck hasn't had time to work yet!"

Wynnie jumped her blue high-tops up the front steps. She opened the door and let it slam behind her. "I'm here," she yelled.

"You don't have to shout," said Mrs. Cadwell, looking in from the kitchen.

"Sorry," said Wynnie. "I keep forgetting. I *don't* have to shout," she said. "This place is the size of a closet. I could whisper in the basement and you'd hear me in the attic. But that's all right!" Wynnie smiled.

Mrs. Cadwell came in from the kitchen, wiping her hands on her jeans. "That's all right?" asked her mother.

"I'm happy," said Wynnie, plopping into the big overstuffed chair.

Mrs. Cadwell sat on the arm of the old chair and

smoothed Wynnie's hair back. "Are you beginning to like Linton?" asked her mother. "Even just a little bit?"

Wynnie shook her head. "No!" she said. "The most mysterious thing about Linton is why *anyone* would want to live here."

Mrs. Cadwell sighed. "Well, *I* want to live here. And I want to live with you," she said, giving Wynnie a quick hug. Wynnie let herself be hugged. "I know you miss your dad and your friends. But this town is full of nice people—people I've known all my life."

Mrs. Cadwell looked into Wynnie's eyes. "What you need is a good friend!" she said.

"I don't want to meet anyone here," said Wynnie.

"Your birthday is coming up," said Mrs. Cadwell. "Who will we invite for your birthday party?"

"I'm not really thinking about my next birthday," said Wynnie, with a little, secret smile. "I'm still thinking about my last birthday." And a certain wish, Wynnie completed the sentence to herself.

There was a knock on the front door. Her mother walked into the tiny kitchen. "Will you get that, please, Wynnie?"

Wynnie pulled herself out of the chair and opened the door. The porch was empty. She stepped out and looked both ways. No one was in sight. Wynnie was about to close the door when she saw it.

A brown box sat on the top step. Wynnie picked it up. She carried it inside, kicking the door shut behind her.

"What's that?" asked Mrs. Cadwell, coming in from the kitchen. "It's too late for the mail."

"It's a package," said Wynnie. She looked closely at the box, turning it one way and then another. "That's funny," she said. "There are no stamps on the box. It didn't come through the mail."

"Well, it didn't just appear on the step," said Mrs. Cadwell.

"Yes," said Wynnie. "It *did*. It just appeared on the step. I looked around. I didn't see anyone who could have left it. But it isn't for us. It's for someone named 'Annabelle Dupree.'"

"I wonder who *she* could be?" asked Mrs. Cadwell.

Wynnie shrugged. "Maybe she used to live in this house," said Wynnie.

"No," said Mrs. Cadwell. "We rented this house from Mr. Gross. He and his wife lived here for 20 years until they moved to Florida. Wait, there's a note," she said, pulling a small pink piece of paper out from under the string that was tied around the package. "Something is waiting for you in the library," Mrs. Cadwell read.

Wynnie took the note from her mother. A sweet

smell drifted up to her. "This note smells like flowers," she said.

"It's perfumed paper," said Mrs. Cadwell.

"What should we do?" asked Wynnie.

"I'd go to the library myself and ask a few questions," said Mrs. Cadwell. "But I haven't got the time. I'll just give the package to the mail carrier on Monday."

"But this package didn't come in the mail. Hopping toad!" exclaimed Wynnie. "This is mysterious." She shook the box, just slightly. No rattles or thumps. "Why don't *I* go to the library," she said. "Maybe someone there will know Annabelle Dupree."

"I'm not sure," said Mrs. Cadwell, thoughtfully. "I think you should spend your time on your homework. You're getting all C's from Mrs. Paine, you know."

"Pigs knuckles and chicken lips, Mom," said Wynnie. "Mrs. Paine gives me a pain! 'Raise your hand before you speak, Wynnie,'" said Wynnie, imitating Mrs. Paine. "'Have you done your homework, Wynnie?'" Wynnie frowned. "Mrs. Paine-in-the-Rumpus! Besides, you're *always* trying to get me to go to the library! Here's your big chance!"

Mrs. Cadwell sighed, then nodded. "All right," she said. "You can go right to the library. And get a good book, as long as you're there!"

"Thanks!" said Wynnie, hugging her mother. Then she ran to her room to change. This called for a new disguise.

"I'll find her," promised Wynnie as she tossed her old disguise on the floor. "Cross my heart and hope to eat tadpoles if I don't!" she said with a smile. She set the box on the table, near the front door.

With a little luck in her pocket, maybe it wasn't too late for her birthday wish to come true after all.

Miss Dulac

The Linton Public Library did not look like a library at all. It was an old, white house set far back from the street.

Wynnie's feet made a hollow sound as she crossed the porch. She pulled the brim of her hat down over one eye. She tipped back her head, ready for what she might find behind the big door. A bell tinkled softly as Wynnie stepped inside and the door closed quietly behind her.

A staircase leading to the second floor was the first thing Wynnie saw. There was rope across it with a sign that said, PLEASE DO NOT GO BEYOND THIS POINT. On the left was a room with a desk, a computer, tables, and shelves full of books. On the right was another room, full of books. There were two long tables with chairs for reading.

"Read to me!" shrieked a strange, high voice.

Wynnie stepped back. "Spitballs!" she gasped.

"Read to me!" the voice screamed again.

A girl at the first table turned to Wynnie with a smile. "It's just Longfellow," she said.

"Who?" asked Wynnie.

"The bird," said the girl. "Over there," she added, pointing. "He's named after a poet."

Wynnie walked around the desk and down a narrow hall, following the sound of the voice. On a perch beside a big bay window sat a bright green parrot.

"Read to me!" the bird said again. "Mary, Mary, quite contrary!" he said, tilting his head to one side and fixing a beady eye on Wynnie.

Wynnie laughed in spite of herself. "The library has a parrot?" she said aloud.

"Yes," said a voice very close behind her.

Wynnie whirled around. A tiny, gray-haired lady stood in the hall, her arms full of books. Her blue eyes crinkled around the edges as she smiled at Wynnie.

"I'm Miss Dulac," said the little woman.

"Miss Du, Miss Du, Miss Du," Longfellow squawked. "Love you, love you, love you."

"If you give him sunflower seeds," said Miss Dulac, "he'll be quiet. The seeds are in that can on the windowsill," she said, nodding toward the right.

Wynnie opened the can and poured seeds into the dish attached to Longfellow's perch.

15

"Little Miss Muffet," said Longfellow. He picked up a sunflower seed and cracked it open with his beak.

"No," said Miss Dulac. "Her name is Wynnie Cadwell."

Wynnie was so surprised she couldn't speak. She opened her mouth but nothing came out. Wynnie trailed Miss Dulac to the front desk. "How do you know my name?"

"I'm interested in people," answered Miss Dulac. "I watch and I listen. And you can't hide for long in a small town. Can I help you find a book?" asked Miss Dulac.

Wynnie shook her head. "I need to ask you a question," she said.

"Excellent!" said Miss Dulac. "Questions are what librarians like best! Fire away!"

"Do you know someone named Annabelle Dupree?" asked Wynnie.

"Annabelle Dupree!" shouted Miss Dulac.

The little girl by the door turned and frowned. "Shh! This is a library," she said.

"So sorry," said Miss Dulac. Now she whispered, "It's just that I found this on my desk when I arrived here this morning."

She handed Wynnie a book. *The Secret Lock,*" Wynnie read from the cover, "by Annabelle Dupree."

"There was a note!" said Miss Dulac. She handed Wynnie a familiar-looking piece of pink paper. Wynnie could smell the sweet flower scent. "Someone will come and pick up this book," read the note. "But make sure she applies for a library card first!"

"Do you know who left this?" asked Wynnie.

Miss Dulac shook her head.

"Could I check out this book?" asked Wynnie.

"Do you have a library card?" asked Miss Dulac.

"No," admitted Wynnie. "But I was going to get one, honest!"

"Good," said Miss Dulac with a sweet smile. "I'll give you one right now."

"Right!" said Wynnie. She turned the book over in her hand. "Maybe there's a clue in the book," she said.

Miss Dulac smiled. "That's for a good detective like yourself to find out," she said.

"Firecrackers! Who told you I was a detective?" asked Wynnie.

Miss Dulac smiled knowingly. "I told you, it's hard to keep a secret in a small town. Just read the book!" she said. "As soon as you fill out this form, you will have your passport to adventure!"

"I'll have my what?" asked Wynnie.

"Your library card," said Miss Dulac.

Card in hand, Wynnie tucked the book under her

arm, and walked out of the library and down the sidewalk. Now she was sure. Her birthday wish *was* coming true. Even Linton was starting to look good as Wynnie walked down First Street. She couldn't wait for the next mysterious thing to happen!

The big mailbox stood by the curb in front of her house. Wynnie sorted through the mail. There was a bright color postcard from her father. "On business in Florida," she read. "Thinking of you. Love, Dad." On the front was a picture of an alligator. Wynnie was so happy she smiled at the alligator.

She walked to the porch. Stopping on the first step, she whirled around, looking up and down the street.

No one was there.

Maybe it was the mysterious package, or the mysterious book under her arm. Or maybe it was just her imagination. But Wynnie had the strange feeling that someone was following her.

The Secret Lock

"Warts!" complained Wynnie. "I don't like to read."

"If you don't read the book," said Mrs. Cadwell as she put away some groceries, "you may miss a clue or a message."

"I suppose you're right," said Wynnie grumpily. She plopped sideways into the big chair. Her legs dangled over the arm.

The pages of the book were brown with age. They smelled like Grandma Cadwell's attic. Wynnie looked at the title page. *The Secret Lock* had been published 40 years ago! "Hen's toes!" exclaimed Wynnie. Forty years was a very long time ago.

She turned another page. "Chapter One," she read aloud. "This better be good!" Wynnie snuggled deeper in the chair and began to read: "It was a small town where nothing exciting ever happened until Mr. Hartly, the mailman found a mysterious note at the bottom of his mailbag. It had just one word written on it. 'Help!'"

A wonderful shiver ran down Wynnie's back. She had the feeling that this was going to be a very good book.

&. &. &.

For the rest of the weekend, Wynnie did everything with *The Secret Lock* in her hand. She ate with the book propped up against the jelly jar at breakfast on Sunday morning. There was a smudge of grape jelly on page 92. She read as her mother combed the snaggles out of her hair before church. Wynnie used the comb as a bookmark on page 113. She even read in the bathtub. Page 132 had a little shampoo in the margin.

Finally, late on Sunday night, she closed the book with a sigh. Her eyes were shining.

"Good book?" asked her mother, leaning over to pull the covers up to her chin and kiss her good night.

"A *great* book," said Wynnie. "It's the best book I've ever read. But it doesn't help. I didn't find a single clue. Who is Annabelle Dupree? Where is she?"

"Think about it in the morning," said Mrs. Cadwell as she turned off the light.

In the morning, Wynnie put her school books and *The Secret Lock* into her backpack.

Boomer Balinski was already in her seat across the

aisle when Wynnie slid into her desk exactly at the sound of the bell. Boomer had just started to say something when Mrs. Paine called the class to order. Mrs. Paine looked down at her students over the top of her glasses. She was a tall woman, and she towered over the class. "It's book report time!" she said. The class groaned.

"Rat's nests!" whispered Wynnie. She hated book reports. But this time she had *The Secret Lock*. It was a book. A *great* book. And she'd already read it!

"In this month's book report, I want each of you to include something about your author," said Mrs. Paine.

"How do we do that?" asked Rusty Pinkas. "My mom won't let me talk to strangers."

Mrs. Paine frowned. "Rusty," she said, sternly. "Please come up here and spend ten minutes in the I-forgot-to-raise-my-hand chair!" She waited as Rusty dawdled his way to the chair at the front of the room.

"Now, class," said Mrs. Paine. "You may write a letter to the company that published the book you read and ask for information about the author. Or you may look in magazines for articles about the author."

"You mean we have to go to the library?" asked Rusty, turning around and holding his hand in the air. The class groaned again.

"Rusty!" warned Mrs. Paine. She looked back at the class. "Libraries can be very interesting places," she told them. "A library can be a treasure chest, a map, a mystery!" she said.

Wynnie sat up straight in her chair. She was really listening now.

"Sometimes a book will have a note about the author at the very end," said Mrs. Paine. "Or you may have to be detectives and really dig to find what you're looking for."

Wynnie grabbed her backpack and dug through it for Annabelle's book. She turned to the last page of the book. "About the Author," she read. Wynnie knocked herself on the forehead. "How could I have missed this?" she muttered under her breath.

Then Wynnie read what it said about Annabelle Dupree: "Annabelle Dupree is the pen name for a very fine first-time author. She loves cooking, teaching, hairstyling, and reading. But most of all, Annabelle Dupree loves a good mystery."

"That's all?" asked Wynnie, right out loud.

Mrs. Paine looked down at Wynnie through her glasses. "If this assignment is not large enough for you, I can give you more work," she said, glaring at Wynnie.

"No," said Wynnie. "I just have a question."

"All right," said Mrs. Paine. "What is it?"

"What's a pen name?" asked Wynnie.

"That's a good question," said Mrs. Paine with surprise. "You must be really thinking today, Wynnie. A pen name is a made-up name used by an author. For example, Mark Twain is the pen name for Samuel Clemens."

"Why doesn't the author use her own name?" asked Wynnie, remembering at the last moment to raise her hand. "If I wrote a book, I'd want the whole world to know that it was mine."

"I don't know," said Mrs. Paine. "You need to ask an author who uses a pen name."

Asking Annabelle Dupree was exactly what Wynnie wanted to do—but first she had to find her! She studied the book again, hoping for a clue. Over the top of the book, she caught Boomer Balinski staring at her.

"Why are you watching me?" whispered Wynnie.

Boomer's face turned almost as pink as her fuzzy sweater. "I don't think I've ever seen you read a book before," Boomer whispered back.

Wynnie shrugged. "How can you do a book report without reading a book?" she asked.

"Rusty Pinkas does it all the time," hissed Boomer.

Wynnie tried to read until she heard something drop onto her desk. It was a note. Boomer smiled and pointed to it. Wynnie took a quick look at Mrs. Paine and opened the note. "Maybe you and I could work together on this book report," were the words Boomer had written inside.

Wynnie sighed. How could little, pink Boomer help her on a real mystery case? She was probably afraid of the dark, afraid to get dirty! Wynnie looked at Boomer and shook her head. "I work alone," she whispered.

Boomer looked very disappointed. "Besides, you wear a lot of pink," said Wynnie, trying to think of something—anything—to make Boomer go away. "I can't get too close to pink."

"Why not?" asked Boomer, sounding insulted.

"If I get too close to pink," said Wynnie, "I just break out in cute all over!"

"Wynnie! Boomer!" said Mrs. Paine. "I believe you have work to do. In fact, since you have time to talk, perhaps you have time to write the spelling words ten times each."

Wynnie hid behind *The Secret Lock* again. She was steaming mad! She knew that Boomer was still watching her. First Wynnie had to find Annabelle Dupree. Then she was going to find a way to lose Boomer Balinski!

After school that afternoon, Wynnie stared at Miss Dulac over the circulation desk. She pushed her dark glasses up on her nose. "Dog biscuits!" she said. "Nobody writes just one book!"

"Just one book," said Miss Dulac, checking the open book. "Annabelle Dupree wrote one book."

"Why didn't she ever write another book? Did something happen to her?" Wynnie gasped. "Do you think . . . did she die?"

Miss Dulac opened *The Secret Lock* to the second page. "There is only one way to find out what really happened to Annabelle Dupree," she said, pointing to the name and address of the publisher. "Write a letter and ask!"

Wynnie pulled out a chair at the table in the biggest room of the library. It was silent except for Longfellow's squawking in the distance.

Wynnie opened her notebook and ripped out a piece of paper. She wrote a letter to the Reilly and Sons Publishing Company in New York City.

Dear Mr. Reilly or Son,

I have a package that belongs to someone named Annabelle Dupree. It came to my house by accident. I didn't know what to do with the package until I found her book The Secret Lock. You published that book 40 years ago. I hope you still remember it. It's the best book I've ever read. What happened to Annabelle Dupree? Why didn't she write another book? Is she still alive? If she is, could she write to me?

I need to know these things and I need to know them fast. I want to deliver the package. Plus, I need this for school. I have to do a book report, and I have to know something about the author. Hurry! I'm already getting C's in just about everything.

Best wishes,
Wynnie Cadwell

P.S. My address is 324 First Street, Linton, Ohio. I used to live somewhere really interesting, but that's another story.

❧   ❧   ❧

That evening, Wynnie's mother gave her an envelope and a stamp. "If you'd like, I'll mail it with my letters on my way to work," said Mrs. Cadwell.

"All right," said Wynnie. "All I can do now is wait. Or I could call Dad and tell him all about it. You know Dad loves a mystery!"

"Yes," said her mother. "And he loves you, too."

Wynnie dialed her father's number and let the phone ring at least a dozen times. Wynnie imagined the phone ringing and ringing in the dark of her father's new apartment. It made her feel lonely. She hung up the phone.

Wynnie wandered into the living room and picked up Annabelle's book. She began to read *The Secret Lock* for the second time. The book had four wonderful detectives and a great secret. It was the best book Wynnie had ever read. She looked at the brown box, sitting on the table by the door.

She really wanted to know what happened to Annabelle Dupree.

The only thing that she wanted more was for her dad to answer the telephone. Had her birthday wish used up all the luck in that four-leaf clover?

The First Clue

Rusty Pinkas was the first one in the class to get a letter from an author. Mrs. Paine put Rusty's letter on the bulletin board.

The next day Arlene Poole got a letter from Pammy Johnson. "She wrote *The Pom-Pom Girls Make Cookies, The Pom-Pom Girls Flunk Math,* and lots of other books," Arlene told the class. "My letter has a card I can send if I want to become a member of the Pom-Pom Girls fan club."

Wynnie shook her head in disgust.

"I don't want to be a Pom-Pom girl," said Boomer later as she and Wynnie worked side by side at the art project table.

"Really?" asked Wynnie. She looked at Boomer in her pink sweater and skirt. "But they dress just like you do," she said, with a shrug. "They have those great *pink* outfits!"

"They don't wear pink for the right reason," said

Boomer.

"What do you mean?" asked Wynnie.

"Why have you started wearing dark glasses and that old raincoat that's too big for you?" asked Boomer.

"To be mysterious, to keep people guessing," said Wynnie.

"Maybe I wear pink and carry a pink purse for the same reason," said Boomer.

"Never," said Wynnie. "What do you carry in that little pink purse, anyway?" she asked.

Boomer smiled. "It's not really a purse," she said. "It's a weapon."

"A weapon!" hooted Wynnie. "Oh, yes, I've heard of lots of people being hurt by purses!" Wynnie snorted and laughed until Mrs. Paine finally heard her and made her sit in the I-cannot-follow-the-class-rules chair for the rest of the day.

❧   ❧   ❧

"Are you making any new friends?" asked her father on the telephone that night.

"No," sighed Wynnie. "But there is one girl named Boomer Balinski."

"Boomer!" laughed her father. "Does she boom when she talks?"

"That's just it," said Wynnie. "She whispers! She wears little pink outfits and carries a little purse. She follows me everywhere."

"Maybe she wants to be your friend," said Mr. Cadwell.

"I don't want ordinary friends like Boomer," said Wynnie. "I'm looking for mysterious people. Brown-paper-bag kind of people who aren't what they look like on the outside. I'm looking for people who understand the art of disguise!"

"Don't forget," said her father. "There are all kinds of disguises. This is a pretty big case. You could use some help searching for Annabelle Dupree."

"I'll work alone," said Wynnie. "Unless *you* want to come and help me," she said, hopefully.

"I wish I *could* help you, Wynnie," said her dad. "But I have work and . . ."

"I know," sighed Wynnie. "I know."

"Well," said her father. "Good luck!"

"That's what I'm hoping for," Wynnie said sadly.

A few days later, three more students in Mrs. Paine's class had letters. Wynnie chewed nervously on the end of her pencil.

"I don't have a letter, yet, either," said Boomer

later, sitting down at the lunch table across from Wynnie. "I've been searching my mailbox every day, just like you."

"What do you mean—just like me?" asked Wynnie.

"Well," said Boomer. "You *do* search your mailbox every day, don't you?"

"Yes," said Wynnie. "But how did *you* know?"

Boomer's face flushed hot pink, then red. "I . . . guessed!" she said. She opened her lunch bag and studied her tuna sandwich very closely.

That afternoon, Wynnie pulled the mailbox door down and reached inside. In the box was just one long, white envelope.

"Miss Wynnie Cadwell," read Wynnie. The envelope had Wynnie's address written on it, but there was no return address.

Wynnie held her breath as she ripped open the letter—the most incredible letter Wynnie had ever seen. It said,

Dear Wynnie,

I am Annabelle Dupree. Yes, I am alive. I am tired sometimes, but I am alive.

You asked so many questions in your letter. I will answer them all. But I often play a game with the young people who write to

*me. They read my book because they like
mysteries. So I give them a real mystery.*

Annabelle Dupree was amazing. A real mystery!
Wynnie read on.

*I will be happy to tell you all the answers
as soon as you find me.*

Wynnie shook her head. "Find her?" she asked.
"How can I find her?" She turned the paper over.

*I will give you clues, of course. Even
Sherlock Holmes had to have clues!*

"Sherlock Holmes!" whispered Wynnie. Sherlock
Holmes was her favorite detective. Wynnie and her
dad used to love to stay up late at night and watch
movies about Sherlock Holmes on television. She
shivered. Sharing popcorn and old movies with her
dad was one of the things she missed the most. A
letter from Annabelle Dupree could never really
make it up to Wynnie. But it *was* exciting news to
tell her dad about.

"Bells and whistles!" sang Wynnie. "Happy Birthday
to me!"

*First you must know who you are looking
for. It does not make sense to look for someone young when your suspect is no longer*

young. But how old do you think I am? Here is your first clue. My age is the number of Sherlock's tales plus your age. Send your reply to me, care of Reilly and Sons Publishing.

Good luck,
Annabelle Dupree

Wynnie folded the letter carefully. It was almost too good to be true!

"It's lucky that Dad and I watched all those old movies together," Wynnie said that night over dinner. "But I don't understand. How can I find out how many stories Sir Arthur Conan Doyle wrote about Sherlock Holmes?" she asked.

"Think about it," said Mrs. Cadwell.

Wynnie shook her head. "Back to the library? Warts, warts, and double warts!" she exclaimed. "This isn't a mystery—it's a plot to make me smart!"

      🔍   🔍   🔍

Wynnie pushed her dark glasses back into place on her nose as she walked into the library the next day.

"Why, Wynnie," said Miss Dulac. "I see by your dark glasses that you are here on detective business."

"Exactly," replied Wynnie. "I have a clue!"

"How exciting!" exclaimed Miss Dulac.

"If you wanted to know something—anything—where would you look first?" asked Wynnie.

Miss Dulac smiled. "The encyclopedia, of course," she said.

"Pepperoni pizza! Of course!" said Wynnie. "I need the *D* volume, for Arthur Conan Doyle. I need the *H* volume, for Sherlock Holmes, and the *M* volume, for mystery—just in case."

Her arms full of books, Wynnie struggled to a table in the reading room. She dropped the books on the table. Brushing her hair back from her face, something caught her eye. A shadow moved!

"French fries!" whispered Wynnie. Goose bumps popped out all over her arms. For days now, Wynnie had had the feeling that she was not alone. She was sure someone was following her. Wynnie crept to the wall, walking on tiptoes, keeping her eyes on the shadow. She slid along the wall then jumped into the doorway.

"Ah ha!" shouted Wynnie to an empty hallway.

An older man at the table in the next room jumped at least a foot off his chair. He glared at Wynnie.

"Along came a spider," screamed Longfellow from his perch in the next room.

Wynnie felt a little foolish. "Sorry," she said to the

man. She shook her head. Someone *had* been there—she was positive. She quickly checked the rest of the other room. Besides the man, two preschoolers were in the corner looking at picture books. Miss Dulac was working at the circulation desk.

There was only one other place to hide. The long, dark steps stretched up to the second floor. As always, a rope hung across the stairs with the sign, PLEASE DO NOT GO BEYOND THIS POINT. The sign was swinging ever so slightly. It looked like it was being blown by a ghostly wind. Wynnie looked up into the dark hall. She wasn't going up there alone.

She went back to the table, looking up often, keeping an eye out for whoever might be watching her. Wynnie opened the first book and found "Doyle, Sir Arthur Conan." She read down the page until she came to this line: "Doyle wrote 56 short stories about Sherlock Holmes and his friend Dr. Watson."

Wynnie opened her notebook. On the first clean page in the notebook, she wrote the number *56*. Then she wrote the number *8*—her age.

Wynnie read on: "Doyle also wrote four *books* about Holmes and Watson."

Wynnie wrote down the number *4*. She added the three numbers together. Sixty-eight. Annabelle Dupree was 68 years old!

Wynnie looked at her watch. She had cracked the first clue from Annabelle Dupree in just one hour! "Hot fudge!" she said happily.

Maybe someday someone would write a book about her! Wynnie Cadwell, great detective!

When the books were back on the shelf, Wynnie went whistling down the sidewalk toward home. She jumped up onto the porch of 324 First Street and unlocked the front door. Throwing her back pack into the chair, she ran to the window and peeked through the curtains.

She waited for a minute, maybe more. Finally, the person who had been following her stepped out from behind a parked car across the street. Wynnie watched as the person opened her back pack and pulled out a notebook.

It was pink, of course.

Clue Number Two

"I was meant to be a detective," Wynnie said, happily. She tore a piece of paper out of her notebook and began to write.

Dear Annabelle Dupree,

> *I have studied clue number one, and I think you are 68 years old, give or take a month or two. Am I right? I hope so.*
>
> *Almost everyone in my class has gotten a letter from a real author. I'm not bringing in your letters until I have solved the mystery. This is an A book report for sure! I know you're worth waiting for. You're not just a real author. You're a real mystery.*
>
> *Maybe someday we'll meet. We could have lunch with my mom and dad. My dad loves a mystery, too. I've told him all about you. My mom is the greatest!*

*I wanted a mystery. But this could take
a while. Don't you want your package?*

*Love,
Wynnie Cadwell*

P.S. How did you know how old I am?

"I'll mail that for you," said Mrs. Cadwell as Wynnie folded the letter and put it into an envelope.

"Annabelle Dupree is 68 years old," Wynnie told her mother. "What do you think she looks like?"

"What do *you* think she looks like?" asked Mrs. Cadwell.

"Tall!" said Wynnie. "Like Mrs. Rockford, the school teacher in the *The Secret Lock*." Wynnie thought for a moment. "Or little and fast on her feet like Miss Bonnie, the librarian from *The Secret Lock*."

Mrs. Cadwell shrugged. "Maybe she's a good cook, like Mrs. Oldham, or owns a beauty parlor, like Miss Dodd," she said.

"Mom!" shouted Wynnie. "How do you know about the other two detectives in *The Secret Lock*?"

Mrs. Cadwell smiled and held up Wynnie's library book. "You're not the only one who can read. It's a good book. And, since it's made you happy again, here's to Annabelle Dupree," said Wynnie's mother, picking up her glass of milk. They clinked glasses.

"*Wherever* she is," said Wynnie. "You know, Mom, you could be a really good detective!"

Mrs. Cadwell didn't say a word. She just smiled.

One week later, another letter came to Wynnie from Annabelle.

Dear Wynnie,

Good work! I am 68 years old—give or take a month or two. Sherlock Holmes himself could not have solved it faster!

You know how old I am.

Now do your homework. Use your brain! Here's the next clue. I can be found in the circle.

Good luck,
Annabelle

Wynnie turned the letter over. That was all. Annabelle had not answered Wynnie's question. "Pigs knuckles!" said Wynnie under her breath. "*What* circle?"

She sat on the front step of 324 First Street and read the letter again. Out of the corner of her eye, Wynnie saw something move. It was pink.

Wynnie folded the letter and put it back into the envelope. "I'm putting an end to this," she thought. She stood up slowly and whistled as she unlocked the front door. She closed the door carefully behind her then dashed madly to the back door.

"Man your battle stations!" she yelled as she raced through the house. She opened the back door and peeked out. Wynnie crossed the porch and looked around the corner, down the side of the house. No one was in sight.

It was Wynnie's lucky day. Boomer Balinski was leaning against the side of 324 First Street. Her back was to Wynnie and she was writing in the pink notebook.

Wynnie's blue high-tops didn't make a sound as she crept down the driveway toward Boomer. Step by step, Wynnie got closer and closer. Finally Wynnie took one big jump and grabbed Boomer from behind.

"Touchdown!" shouted Wynnie as Boomer struggled and kicked.

Then, out of nowhere, something hit Wynnie over the head. She let go and sat down hard. She rubbed her head and blinked her eyes. "What did you do?" she asked.

"I hit you with my purse,"said Boomer. "My little, pink purse."

Boomer Balinski wasn't whispering any more.

Partners—Like It or Not

"You hit me!" shouted Wynnie.

"You *grabbed* me!" said Boomer.

"You *followed* me!" said Wynnie.

"I *had* to," said Boomer. "I've decided to be a detective, and I'm working on a big case right now."

"You *can't* be a detective," said Wynnie, standing up and brushing the dirt off her pants. "*I'm* a detective, and anyway, you're so . . . so *pink!*"

Boomer smiled. "It's a pretty good disguise, isn't it?" she said.

Wynnie's mouth dropped open in surprise. "What's this big case," asked Wynnie, "and what does it have to do with me?"

"I don't really know," said Boomer.

"Some detective *you* are!" said Wynnie. "You're following me and you don't know why?"

"All right, so this is my first case," said Boomer. "But I *do* know why I'm following you!" She unzipped

46

her backpack and pulled out a note. A note written on pink paper.

Wynnie sniffed the note. It smelled sweet, just like her notes. She opened it. "If you love a mystery, follow Wynnie Cadwell wherever she goes," read Wynnie. "Signed—someone else who loves mysteries."

"Rooster toes!" gasped Wynnie. "Do you love mysteries?"

Boomer nodded. "I read mysteries all the time. I check them out of the library, and I write book reports about them."

"So you followed me?" asked Wynnie.

"I was going to stop," said Boomer. "But you kept doing interesting things. I couldn't help it," she said. "I kept following you. By the way, what *are* you doing?"

Wynnie tapped the pink note against her hand and took a long look at Boomer. Boomer's ribbons where coming out and her pink shirt was dirty from hiding behind cars and trees. She looked almost human. "Come with me," she said.

Inside the house, Wynnie handed Boomer her pink notes. Boomer read them and then sniffed for herself.

"It's lilac," said Boomer. "My grandma grows lilac bushes in her yard. Every summer, the whole yard smells like lilacs."

"The same person who sent a package to Annabelle

Dupree told you to follow me," said Wynnie. "And left a book at the library, too. What does it mean? And where *is* Annabelle Dupree."

"I don't know," said Boomer. "I'd like to find out. We could—ah—work together and find out."

Wynnie shook her head. "I work alone," she said.

"I know," said Boomer. "But I could help you," she said. "I can't tell you anything about the circle, but I can tell you something about *The Secret Lock*. I've wanted to say something about that book ever since I saw you reading it in class!"

"What is it?" asked Wynnie.

"Wait a minute," said Boomer. "I'm not telling you anything unless you make me a partner on this case."

"That's blackmail!" said Wynnie. "You're not as pink as you look."

"I know this town, and you're new here," said Boomer. "I could save you a lot of time."

Wynnie looked at Boomer's grimy pink outfit and her surprisingly hard pink purse. She thought about what her father had said. She could use a little help. "Goat's lips and sauerkraut! I guess we're partners. What do you know?"

"First, we go to my Grandma Balinski's house," said Boomer, straightening out her clothes.

"Why?" asked Wynnie.

"Number one, because I'm hungry and it's bread baking day,"said Boomer. "And number two, there's something at her house that you need to see."

"This better be good," said Wynnie. "And it better not be pink!"

But it *was* pink, of course.

The Cut and Curl

Grandma Balinski's pink house was just one block from Miss Dulac's library.

The kitchen was full of wonderful smells. Grandma Balinski was a wearing blue jeans and a sweatshirt. Her hands were covered in flour. "You're just in time," she said to the girls as they came in the back door. "I'm working on the sourdough bread now, but the honey wheat will be out in two minutes."

"Grandma," said Boomer. "This is Wynnie Cadwell."

"Nice to meet you, Wynnie," Grandma Balinski said.

"If it's all right, we'll go into the living room," said Boomer. "I want to show Wynnie something."

"Go right ahead," said Grandma, slapping and pounding the bread dough on a wood board.

Boomer pushed through the swinging door that divided the kitchen and the dining room. Beyond the dining room was the living room with tall book-cases, full of books.

"This is what I wanted to show you," said Boomer. She pulled a chair close to the tallest bookcase. Standing on top of the chair, Boomer stretched up and pulled a very familiar book off the top shelf.

"It's *The Secret Lock*!" said Wynnie. "Cheese Doodles!"

"That's what I wanted to tell you about *The Secret Lock*," said Boomer. "Mrs. Paine has a copy of it on the shelf at school. Grandma Balinski has two! See?" she asked, reaching for the second book.

"Careful," said Wynnie, as the chair tipped one way and then the other. "Something fell out of the book," she said, picking up an old picture off the floor.

Boomer climbed down and took the picture from Wynnie. It showed four young women. "This is very old," said Boomer. "It was taken in front of the Cut and Curl Salon," she said.

"You mean the beauty parlor on Main Street?" asked Wynnie.

Boomer nodded. "Grandma Balinski has her hair done there every Wednesday afternoon."

Wynnie took the picture and turned it over. "There are names on the back," she said. "It says Anna Atkins . . ."

"She's the lady who owns the Cut and Curl," said Boomer.

"And the next lady is Alice Preber," said Wynnie.

"That's Grandma Balinski," said Boomer excitedly, "before she married Grandpa."

"And Marie Dulac," said Wynnie. "That's Miss Dulac, from the library, only very young."

"Who's the last lady?" asked Boomer.

"It says Belle—oh, no!" shouted Wynnie.

"Belle who?" asked Boomer.

Wynnie shook her head. "It says Belle Paine," said Wynnie. "It's Mrs. Paine, our teacher."

"That's funny," said Boomer. "Mrs. Paine and Miss Dulac have their hair done every Wednesday afternoon with Grandma Balinski. Do you think this picture has something to do with Annabelle Dupree?"

"Of course not," said Wynnie. "What would four ladies from Linton have to do with an author?"

Wynnie shook her head. "We don't have time to think about this right now. We have to find the circle. I think we should go to the library."

"What will we do there?" asked Boomer.

Wynnie shrugged. "I'm not sure," she said. "But I've learned that there's a little bit of everything in a library."

Boomer shook her head. "I think you're wrong," she said. "I mean, I know there's a little bit of everything in a library, but this picture may be a clue. And

I know where we can find a lot more just like it."

"Where?" asked Wynnie.

Boomer pointed straight up. "The attic," said Boomer. "I've been up there before. Grandma has old pictures and even more books up there."

Wynnie thought for a moment. "I think you're right," she said.

"Good," said Boomer. "Let's go!"

"Not so fast!" hissed Wynnie. "We can't let anyone know what we're doing!"

Boomer thought for a moment. "I *could* ask if you and I could spend the night here tonight. It's Friday. We could wait until Grandma goes to bed and then go up to the attic and look around."

"Perfect!" said Wynnie. "Detectives love late night work."

As they ate a slice of bread warm from the oven, Boomer and Grandma Balinski talked and made plans for Boomer and Wynnie to spend the night. When Wynnie called home to ask permission to stay, her mom sounded surprised but pleased. Afterward, Boomer and Grandma Balinski talked about making up beds in the spare bedroom and finding a nightgown for Wynnie.

Wynnie was too busy thinking to talk.

It was that name. Belle. Belle Paine. It sounded a

lot like Annabelle. Wynnie smiled over her secret joke. Mrs. Paine was cranky. Mrs. Paine *was* a pain. Mrs. Paine could never be Annabelle Dupree and write a mystery that sent shivers up Wynnie's back!

Or could she?

A *Real* Dark and Stormy Night

"Finally," Wynnie told Boomer happily. "It really *is* a dark and stormy night!" She reached into the bowl of popcorn that sat on the window seat between them. Outside the window, rain poured down and lightning streaked across the sky. Every once in a while, thunder would rumble.

Boomer tucked her pink flannel nightgown around her feet. She looked to be sure Grandma Balinski was still in the kitchen. "Maybe we shouldn't go up there tonight," said Boomer. "It *is* awfully dark and there's only one small light."

"I knew it!" said Wynnie. "I knew you were too pink to do the detective D-work!"

"What's D-work?" asked Boomer.

"Daring and Dangerous," said Wynnie. "That's *real* detective work."

Boomer frowned. "I'm not afraid of those D's," she said. "It's the *other* D's I'm worried about!"

55

"What other D's?" asked Wynnie.

"Dirty and Dark!" shouted Boomer.

"Shhh!" hissed Wynnie.

"It will be cold and dark up there," whispered Boomer. "And it's covered with dust and cobwebs."

"Sherlock Holmes wasn't afraid of cobwebs, and neither am I!" said Wynnie, folding her arms across her chest. "I'll just have to go alone."

Boomer shook her head. "I'll go," she said. "But there won't be anything there at night that isn't there during the day!"

"Yes, there will," said Wynnie. "We'll be there!"

Later that night the big clock downstairs struck 11 times. Boomer slowly opened the door of Grandma Balinski's spare bedroom. "I think she's asleep," whispered Boomer.

Wynnie stood behind her, a flashlight Boomer had found for her in her hand. She nodded. "Let's go," she whispered.

"I don't think this is a good idea," said Boomer.

"Then don't think," said Wynnie. "Just follow a *real* detective!"

The two detectives crept to the door at the end of the hall. Suddenly, a board creaked. They froze, holding their breath. They could hear rain hitting the roof above their heads. But Grandma Balinski did not appear.

Wynnie held her finger to her lips and pointed to the door. They kept walking. Finally they reached the door and opened it silently.

"The light is at the top of the stairs," whispered Boomer.

They climbed the stairs, the flashlight lighting their way. At the very top, Boomer climbed on top of a box and reached for the string that hung down from one, bare light bulb up near the ceiling. She pulled the string.

Nothing happened.

"What's wrong?" asked Wynnie.

"I guess the bulb is burned out," said Boomer. "It doesn't work."

Wynnie looked around the attic. It was very dark. The flashlight's tiny light was too small to make a real difference. "We'll have to try again," said Wynnie. "We'll find a light bulb and bring it with us, next time."

Very quietly, Boomer sighed with relief. They crept back down the dark stairs. Boomer turned the knob on the door and pushed. It didn't move.

"What's the matter?" asked Wynnie.

"It's locked," hissed Boomer. "What are we going to do?"

Wynnie thought for a moment. "We'll go back up

and look for a key or a screwdriver or a hairpin," she said. "Anything that we can use to open the door and not tell Grandma Balinski what we're up to!"

Back up the stairs they went.

Wynnie began to search the attic with the help of the tiny light. "Do you have to get so close?" asked Wynnie, stepping on Boomer's toes.

"*You're* the one with the flashlight," said Boomer, looking at the dark and strange shapes all around her.

"Do you see a tool box?" asked Wynnie.

"I can't see anything," said Boomer.

Suddenly lightning flashed in the tiny window at the other end of the attic. In the brief bright light the girls could see someone standing in the corner of the attic! Boomer screamed! Shaking, Wynnie pointed the flashlight at the tall figure. They both stared and then sighed with relief. It was just a dressmaker's dummy.

Wynnie shook her head and went on looking. "There are a million books in here," she said, shining the light on stacks of dusty books.

"Oh!" she gasped. "Oh, my goodness!"

"What is it?" asked Boomer. "It's not a mouse is it?"

"It's *The Secret Lock*," said Wynnie. She handed a book to Boomer.

"You mean that Grandma Balinski has *three* copies of *The Secret Lock*?" asked Boomer.

"No," said Wynnie. "She doesn't have three copies—she has at least *fifty* copies!" Wynnie pointed to the box.

Boomer looked into the box and shook her head. "Why would she have so many copies of Annabelle's book?" she asked.

"Maybe *she* is Annabelle," said Wynnie.

"No!" cried Boomer, "she is *not* Annabelle! She's not a writer, and she would never send a mystery to you through the mail! She's not mysterious or even tricky! I beat her at checkers all the time!"

"Maybe that's *her* disguise," said Wynnie.

"No," repeated Boomer. "My grandma is not part of your stupid game. I don't want to talk about it any more!"

"A detective can't stop listening," said Wynnie. "A detective has to look at *all* the facts."

Boomer's arms were crossed, and she was staring at Wynnie with a frown on her face.

"Oh, I give up!" said Wynnie. "You'll never understand. I can't wait until I get back to the city. That's where my dad lives, and he understands detective work."

"When are you moving back to the city?" asked Boomer.

"Soon," said Wynnie. "I'll go back and live with my dad. He wants me to live with him."

"Why did you come to Linton at all?" sniffed

Boomer. "Why didn't you just stay in the city?"

"That is not *your* business," said Wynnie. "We are supposed to be solving a case. And I'd better keep working, since I seem to be working alone!"

"I can't help you find Annabelle Dupree when you're looking in the wrong place!" stormed Boomer. "And I don't think you're going to live in the city, either!"

"I'm going to live with my dad and we're going to solve great mysteries, big cases," said Wynnie. "After all, I have this mystery, don't I? I *wished* for this mystery."

"What makes you think this is your mystery?" asked Boomer angrily. "Maybe it's *my* mystery. After all, I followed you. The note came to *me*!"

"But the package came to *me*!" said Wynnie. "I don't need you on this case. I'll find Annabelle Dupree. I'll find the *real* Annabelle, no matter who she is!"

"Maybe *I'll* find Annabelle without *you*!" said Boomer.

"Fine," said Wynnie. "Forget being partners!"

Wynnie whirled around and ran over to the top of the stairs. "I'm getting out!" She ran right into the arms of a big, white ghost.

Wynnie screamed.

The Circle

Grandma Balinski poured more warm milk into Wynnie's cup. "I'm sorry that I scared you," she said. "I always wear my white flannel nightgown on rainy, cold nights. And you two frightened me! My, I was worried when I heard someone scream in my attic!"

Boomer shook her head. "You sure looked like a ghost, Grandma," she said. "It was so dark up there."

"May I ask why you were in the attic?" asked Grandma Balinski.

Wynnie looked at Boomer. "We . . . ah . . . " Wynnie stopped.

"We were playing a game," said Boomer. "We were going to come back down when the light wouldn't work, but I bumped into a box. That's why I screamed."

"Next time," said Grandma Balinski, "you might want to wait until morning to play a game. Now, off to bed . . . again!"

The two girls walked slowly upstairs. Grandma Balinski stayed behind to rinse milky cups and turn out the lights.

"Thanks for not telling," Wynnie said.

"It doesn't mean that I'm going to be your partner again," said Boomer. "I've decided to work alone."

"That's fine by me," said Wynnie, getting mad all over again.

Nothing seemed to be working. No pieces to the puzzle fit together. Was this really her birthday wish? Would good luck bring her mother and father to the same place? Could they all be together again?

&&   &&   &&

Nothing was any clearer on Monday morning—least of all Wynnie's eyes. The mystery of Annabelle Dupree was making it very hard to sleep.

Boomer was already at her desk when Wynnie stumbled into class. Boomer looked terrible. Even her pink bows were droopy and crooked.

Francine Stewart had her author's letter to share with the class. Wynnie didn't even listen.

After tacking Francine's letter to the bulletin board, Mrs. Paine stepped into the hall to speak to Mrs. Barkley, who was the school's principal.

Francine sat near Boomer and Wynnie. "I got a

great letter, didn't I?" chattered Francine. "I'm going to keep it forever. It's the first letter I've ever gotten from New York City." Francine gazed at the envelope. "See?" she said, holding the envelope out to Wynnie. "The postmark says New York City."

Wynnie looked at the envelope and then grabbed it out of Francine's hands.

"Give that back!" exclaimed Francine.

"I will! I will! In a minute," said Wynnie. Then she leaned across the aisle. "Boomer!" she hissed.

Boomer didn't answer.

"Boomer," said Wynnie, holding the envelope out for Boomer to see. "Look at the postmark on Francine's letter," she said.

"It's lovely," said Boomer. "It's the prettiest postmark I have ever seen. Don't speak to me." She opened her spelling book and pretended to be very interested in it.

"Boomer," whispered Wynnie. "I'm sorry. I didn't like the questions you asked about my dad. But this is a mystery. It's mine . . . *and* yours. I don't want to find Annabelle Dupree all alone."

Boomer peeked up over the edge of the book. "I found another clue yesterday," she said. "I wasn't going to tell you about it. But maybe I will."

"Good!" said Wynnie. "But first, listen to me! Mrs.

Paine will be back in a second. Postmarks tell you where a letter was mailed. They tell you *where someone lives*! And they are round."

"Like a circle!" Boomer whispered. Her eyes were round, too.

Without a word Wynnie pulled her backpack out from under her desk. She searched until she found one of Annabelle's letters. Then she stared at the red postmark in the corner.

"What does it say?" asked Boomer.

Wynnie shook her head, not believing her eyes.

Annabelle Dupree lived in Linton.

The most boring town in the world.

She handed the envelope to Boomer, who studied it without a word.

"What's *your* clue?" asked Wynnie.

Boomer's face was white. "I went back to my grandma's house yesterday," she said. "I found this in the desk drawer in the guest room." Boomer pulled out a sheet of familiar pink paper.

Wynnie knew, even without the sniff test, that it would smell like lilacs.

Finding Annabelle and Something More

Later, Wynnie and Boomer sat alone at lunch. "Hot tamales!" said Wynnie. "This changes everything."

"Why? Anybody could have that paper. They sell it at the drug store," said Boomer. "Annabelle Dupree lives in Linton. Let's write and tell her that we've found her!"

"But I want to *really* find her," said Wynnie. "Sherlock Holmes always walks in and says, 'That's the crook!' Well, I want to walk in and say, 'That's the author!'"

Boomer shook her head. "How do we do that?" she asked.

"I don't know," said Wynnie. "If my dad were here . . . he'd know what to do."

Boomer looked down. "I'm sorry I made you mad," she said. "I mean, when I asked about your dad."

"It's all right," said Wynnie. "He writes and calls all the time. But he seems so far away. Why can't he be here? I want my mom *and* my dad. I thought if I had a mystery to solve, maybe he would want to come live in Linton, too. I wonder if he thinks of me as much as I think of him?"

"Sure he thinks about you," said Boomer. "My mom always tells me to make a list if I'm ever in doubt about something. I'll bet if you made a list—wrote down all the things your dad has done for you—you would see that he loves you a lot and thinks about you all the time."

Wynnie smiled. "That's it!" she said.

"*What's* it?" asked Boomer.

"A list," said Wynnie.

Wynnie reached for Boomer's notebook. "We're going to make a list of all the facts, all the things we *know* about Annabelle Dupree."

Boomer smiled. "Right!" she said. "Where do we start?"

"Start with what's in the back of *The Secret Lock*," said Wynnie. She started to write.

> Annabelle Dupree is a pen name. A made-up name.
> She loves to cook, teach, style hair, and read.
> She is 68 years old.
> She wrote only one book.

"And now we know that she lives in Linton," said Boomer. "And it may be someone we already know. But who?"

"It sounds like Mrs. Paine," said Wynnie, with a sigh. "She must be at *least* that old. And the name is almost the same."

"She doesn't style hair," said Boomer. "And she doesn't cook! Remember, she once told us she *hates* to cook. It's funny," she said. "This *does* sound like Grandma Balinski. She loves to cook. And read."

"But she doesn't teach or style hair," said Wynnie.

Wynnie stared at the clues. "Do you remember all the names of the ladies in front of the Cut and Curl Salon?" she asked. "The ladies in the picture?"

Boomer nodded. "Anna Atkins, Alice Preber, Marie Dulac, and Belle Paine."

Wynnie wrote the names at the bottom of the page. "That's funny," she said. "There's an Anna and a Belle, but not an Annabelle." She looked at the names a little while longer.

"Oh!" said Boomer suddenly.

Boomer grabbed the notebook from Wynnie's hands. She wrote the names again, in a different order. She handed the notebook back to Wynnie. Wynnie studied the names, and then she smiled.

"Do you think we're right?" asked Boomer.

Wynnie nodded. "We're right. And we're a lot better detectives than they thought." Wynnie smiled at Boomer. "We're a good team," she said.

"But you've got a lot to learn about disguises," said Boomer. "And I have a lot to learn about grandmas!"

And quiet, little, pink Boomer Balinski boomed with laughter.

What Really Happened to Annabelle Dupree

"Your mom won't worry, will she?" asked Boomer, as they hurried down Main Street two days later.

Wynnie shifted Annabelle Dupree's package to her other arm. "I told her I was going to the Cut and Curl Salon because we've found Annabelle Dupree."

"Was she surprised?" asked Boomer.

"I think she was very surprised," said Wynnie. "She said she was glad that I'd found a partner."

A bell on the salon door rang as Boomer and Wynnie walked in.

Mrs. Atkins was cutting Mrs. Paine's hair. Miss Dulac was under a hair dryer. Grandma Balinski's hair was set in a hundred little pink rollers.

"Hello, Wynnie," called Miss Dulac. "What's in the box?" she asked.

"We've been trying to find the owner of this package and the author of this book," said Wynnie, holding up her copy of *The Secret Lock*. "And we've found her."

70

"Really?" asked Miss Dulac, turning off the dryer.

"She's 68 years old, lives in Linton, loves cooking, teaching, hair styling, and reading. I don't know why she wrote only one book. Annabelle Dupree will have to answer that question," said Wynnie.

"And who is Annabelle Dupree?" asked Mrs. Paine.

"You are," said Wynnie, looking at Mrs. Paine. "You love to teach."

"And so are you, Grandma," said Boomer. "You're the cook."

"And you're Annabelle, Mrs. Atkins," said Wynnie. "You're the one who styles hair. And we don't want to forget *you,* Miss Dulac. You're the one who loves to read. You are *all* Annabelle Dupree. Anna, Belle, Dulac and Preber put together in a pen name."

The women looked at each other and smiled.

"Open the package," said Mrs. Paine.

"Me?" asked Wynnie. "You want *me* to open the package?"

"Yes," giggled Miss Dulac. "And hurry!"

Wynnie looked at Boomer and shrugged. She pulled the string off the box and looked inside. It was full of paper, wadded up and stuffed around a small jewelry box. Wynnie opened the box. Inside was a gold chain with a tiny gold key. A pink note was folded under the key. "Happy Birthday, Wynnie" said the note. "You have unlocked the secret. Love, Dad."

From a room in the back of the salon came the sound of singing. Someone was singing "Happy Birthday to You."

Mrs. Cadwell stepped out of the back room, followed by Mrs. Balinski, Boomer's mother. She carried a cake with nine candles across the top. "Happy Birthday, Dear Wynnie," they sang.

Everyone was smiling at Wynnie and Boomer.

"You wanted a mystery for your birthday, Wynnie," said Mrs. Cadwell. "Your dad wanted to give you one."

"*He* made a mystery?" asked Wynnie. "Just for me?"

"Just for you!" said her mother. "And we all helped with the plan. He may be far away, but he loves you very much."

Wynnie slipped the chain around her neck. She pressed the tiny key in her hand.

"I wanted you to give you a friend for your birthday," said Mrs. Cadwell. "You were spending too much time alone. So I called *my* best friend from the third grade. Together we planned a mystery *and* a chance to find a friend as well."

"Who's your best friend from the third grade?" asked Wynnie.

"Me!" said Mrs. Balinski. "I thought of the book

Grandma Balinski and her friends had written. We all made up a mystery, but you two were so good—you found a lot more than we planned."

"That picture of the four of us wasn't part of the plan at all!" said Grandma Balinski.

"How did you know that I found the picture?" asked Boomer.

"I was spying on you in the living room," Grandma Balinski said.

"Grandmothers can be very mysterious people," said Mrs. Atkins.

"So can librarians," said Miss Dulac.

"So can mothers," said Mrs. Cadwell. "I never mailed your letters at all, Wynnie. I used them to help make new plans!"

"Are you really all Annabelle Dupree?" asked Boomer.

"Oh, yes," said Miss Dulac. "We have loved mysteries ever since we were little girls together. We grew up together here in Linton."

"We read mysteries all the time," said Mrs. Paine.

"We never dreamed we would write one. Then we read about a mystery-writing contest from a magazine right here in the Cut and Curl," said Miss Dulac. "We knew we could win that contest. We decided to write together every Wednesday afternoon."

"Only one person could enter the contest," said Mrs. Atkins. "It was Belle's idea to create a pen name."

"Why didn't you write another book?" asked Wynnie.

"It was fun to write the book," said Grandma Balinski, "but it was also hard work."

"Our lives changed. We had more important things to do," said Miss Dulac. "I loved my library. I loved giving people their passports to adventure."

"That's a library card," Wynnie told Boomer.

"My business was taking off," said Mrs. Atkins. "I liked my little shop on the Main Street of the best little town in the world!"

"I got married," said Grandma Balinski. "And then I had a baby. Your dad!"

Boomer laughed.

"And I wanted to teach," said Mrs. Paine. "I wanted to teach children to try harder and reach higher, even if I give them a pain sometimes."

Wynnie turned pink.

"But this is A work, Wynnie and Boomer," said Mrs. Paine. "It's the work I *knew* you could do. That's why I wanted to be a part of this mystery," she said. "And I want your book report *with* something about the author on my desk in the morning."

"What will you say about Annabelle Dupree?" asked Grandma Balinski.

"I'll say that you can't tell a book by its cover. And you can't tell people by their outsides, either. People aren't always what they seem," said Wynnie.

"We are good at disguises," said Mrs. Paine.

"The outside may be fancy or," laughed Boomer, "a plain, *pink* paper bag."

"It's time for a birthday wish," said Mrs. Cadwell.

"Do you have a wish?" asked Boomer.

"I *was* going to wish for a friend," said Wynnie. "But why wish for something I already have?" She smiled at Boomer, pink ribbons and all.

"But I *do* have a new wish," said Wynnie.

Wynnie closed her eyes, took a deep breath, and blew out all nine candles.

"What did you wish for?" asked Boomer.

"I can't tell," said Wynnie. "It's a mystery!"